Usborne Farmyard Tales

THE HUNGRY DONKEY

Heather Amery

Illustrated by Stephen Cartwright

Language Consultant: Betty Root
Reading and Language Information Centre
University of Reading, England

There is a little yellow duck to find on every page.

This is Apple Tree Farm.

This is Mrs Boot, the farmer. She has two children called Poppy and Sam, and a dog called Rusty.

There is a donkey on the farm.

The donkey is called Ears. She lives in a field with lots of grass, but she is always hungry.

3

Ears, the donkey, is going out.

Poppy and Sam catch Ears and take her to the farmyard. Today is the day of the Show.

4

Ears has a little cart.

They brush her coat, comb her tail and clean her feet. Mrs Boot puts her into her little cart.

Off they go to the Show.

Poppy and Sam climb up into the little cart. They all go down the lane to the show ground.

"You stay here, Ears."

At the show ground, Mrs Boot ties Ears to a
fence. "Stay here. We'll be back soon," she says.

7

Ears gets free.

Ears is hungry and bored with nothing to do. She pulls and pulls on the rope until she is free.
8

Ears looks for food.

Ears trots across the field to the show ring. She sees a bunch of flowers and some fruit.

"That looks good to eat."

She takes a big bite, but the flowers do not taste very nice. A lady screams and Ears is frightened.
10

Ears runs away.

Mrs Boot, Poppy and Sam and the lady run after her and catch her. "Naughty donkey," says Sam.

Ears is in disgrace.

"I'm sorry," Mrs Boot says to the lady. "Would you like to take Ears into the best donkey competition?"

Ears is very good now.

The lady is called Mrs Rose. She climbs into the cart. "Come on," she says and shakes the reins.

Ears trots into the show ring.

She trots round the ring, pulling the cart. She stops and goes when Mrs Rose tells her.

Ears wins a prize.

"Well done," says the judge and gives her a
rosette. He gives Mrs Rose a prize too. It is a hat.

It is time to go home.

Mrs Rose waves goodbye. "That was such fun,"
she says. Ears trots home. She has a new hat too.

First published in 1990 by Usborne Publishing Ltd, Usborne House, 83-85 Saffron Hill, London EC1N 8RT, England. Copyright © 1990 Usborne Publishing Ltd.

The name Usborne and the device 🎈 are Trade Marks of Usborne Publishing Ltd. All rights reserved. No part of this publication may be reproduced, stored in a retrieval system or transmitted by any form or by any means, electronic, mechanical, photocopy, recording or otherwise, without the prior permission of the publisher.
Printed in Portugal.